THE 512 Ants
ON SULLIVAN STREET

WARNING: This Book Contains Math— And It's FUN!

by Carol A. Losi
Illustrated by Patrick Merrell
Math Activities by Marilyn Burns

SCHOLASTIC

I, _____,
   (Your Name)

have read this book

❑ once

❑ twice

❑ again and again!

Hello, Math Reader!
Read good stories! Have fun with math!
Look for these great books!

Level 1
❑ MONSTER MATH

Level 2
❑ HOW MANY FEET? HOW MANY TAILS?
❑ JUST A MINUTE
❑ THE SILLY STORY OF GOLDIE LOCKS
   AND THE THREE SQUARES
❑ SLOWER THAN A SNAIL
❑ STAY IN LINE

Level 3
❑ THE BIGGEST FISH
❑ EVEN STEVEN AND ODD TODD
❑ THE LUNCH LINE
❑ A QUARTER FROM THE TOOTH FAIRY

Level 4
❑ THE CASE OF THE MISSING BIRTHDAY PARTY
❑ HOW MUCH IS THAT GUINEA PIG IN THE WINDOW?

There are more great books on the inside back cover!

A Note to Parents

For many children, learning math is difficult and "I hate math!" is their first response — to which many parents silently add "Me, too!" Children often see adults comfortably reading and writing, but they rarely have such models for mathematics. And math fear can be catching!

The easy-to-read stories in this **Hello Math** series were written to give children a positive introduction to mathematics, and parents a pleasurable re-acquaintance with a subject that is important to everyone's life. **Hello Math** stories make mathematical ideas accessible, interesting, and fun for children. The activities and suggestions at the end of each book provide parents with a hands-on approach to help children develop mathematical interest and confidence.

Enjoy the mathematics!
• Give your child a chance to retell the story. The more familiar children are with the story, the more they will understand its mathematical concepts.
• Use the colorful illustrations to help children "hear and see" the math at work in the story.
• Treat the math activities as games to be played for fun. Follow your child's lead. Spend time on those activities that engage your child's interest and curiosity.
• Activities, especially ones using physical materials, help make abstract mathematical ideas concrete.

Learning is a messy process. Learning about math calls for children to become immersed in lively experiences that help them make sense of mathematical concepts and symbols.

Although learning about numbers is basic to math, other ideas, such as identifying shapes and patterns, measuring, collecting and interpreting data, reasoning logically, and thinking about chance, are also important. By reading these stories and having fun with the activities, you will help your child enthusiastically say "**Hello, Math,**" instead of "I hate math."

—Marilyn Burns
National Mathematics Educator
Author of *The I Hate Mathematics! Book*

For Mark and the gang
— C.L.

To Ant Dorothy and Ant Helen
— P.M.

Copyright © 1997 by Scholastic Inc.
The activities on pages 42-48 copyright ©1997 by Marilyn Burns.
All rights reserved. Published by Scholastic Inc.
HELLO MATH READER and CARTWHEEL BOOKS and associated logos
are trademarks and/or registered trademarks of Scholastic Inc.

Library of Congress Cataloging-in-Publication Data is available.

Losi, Carol A.
    The 512 ants on Sullivan Street / by Carol A. Losi; illustrated by
Patrick Merrell; math activities by Marilyn Burns.
        p.   cm. — (Hello math reader. Level 4)
    Summary: In this rhyming, cumulative story, the number of ants doubles each
time they take a new treat from a picnic lunch.
    ISBN 0-590-30876-9
    [1 . Multiplication — Fiction. 2. Ants — Fiction. 3. Picnicking — Fiction.
    4. Stories in rhyme.]
    I. Patrick Merrell, ill. II. Burns, Marilyn III. Title. IV. Series.
PZ8.3.L9115Aal   1997
[E] — dc20   97-5295
                                                                              CIP
                                                                              AC

10 9 8 7 6 5 4 3

Printed in the U.S.A.   24
First printing, August 1997

THE
512 Ants
ON SULLIVAN STREET

by Carol A. Losi
Illustrated by Patrick Merrell
Math Activities by Marilyn Burns

Hello Math Reader — Level 4

SCHOLASTIC INC.
New York   Toronto   London   Auckland   Sydney

This is the basket with goodies to eat

that we packed for a picnic on Sullivan Street.

This is 1 ant who carried a crumb,

a crumb from the basket with goodies to eat

that we packed for a picnic on Sullivan Street.

These are 2 ants with some pieces of plum.

They followed 1 ant who carried a crumb,

a crumb from the basket with goodies to eat

that we packed for a picnic on Sullivan Street.

There go 4 ants with a barbecued chip.

They held it above them so they wouldn't trip.

They trailed the 2 ants with some pieces of plum,

who followed 1 ant who carried a crumb,

a crumb from the basket with goodies to eat

that we packed for a picnic on Sullivan Street.

Here come 8 ants with a crisp bacon strip.

They chased the 4 ants with a barbecued chip,

who trailed the 2 ants with some pieces of plum,

who followed 1 ant who carried a crumb,

a crumb from the basket with goodies to eat

that we packed for a picnic on Sullivan Street.

Now 16 ants took a hard-boiled egg.

They rolled it along with a kick from each leg.

They followed 8 ants with a crisp bacon strip,
who chased the 4 ants with a barbecued chip,
who trailed the 2 ants with some pieces of plum,
who followed 1 ant who carried a crumb,
a crumb from the basket with goodies to eat
that we packed for a picnic on Sullivan Street.

Then 32 ants hauled a wing and a leg.

They trailed 16 ants with a hard-boiled egg,

who followed 8 ants with a crisp bacon strip,

who chased the 4 ants with a barbecued chip,

who trailed the 2 ants with some pieces of plum,

who followed 1 ant who carried a crumb,

a crumb from the basket with goodies to eat

that we packed for a picnic on Sullivan Street.

These 64 ants spied some take-out Chinese.

They carried the white paper carton with ease.

They chased the 32 with a wing and a leg,

who trailed the 16 with a hard-boiled egg,

who followed the 8 with a crisp bacon strip,

who chased the 4 ants with a barbecued chip,

who trailed the 2 ants with some pieces of plum,

who followed 1 ant who carried a crumb,

a crumb from the basket with goodies to eat

that we packed for a picnic on Sullivan Street.

Now 128 ants grabbed some cheese,

and trailed the 64 with the take-out Chinese,

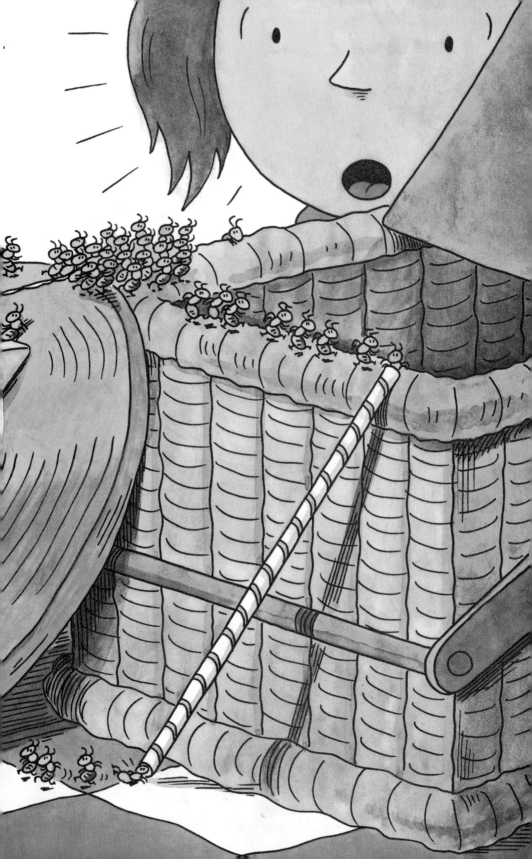

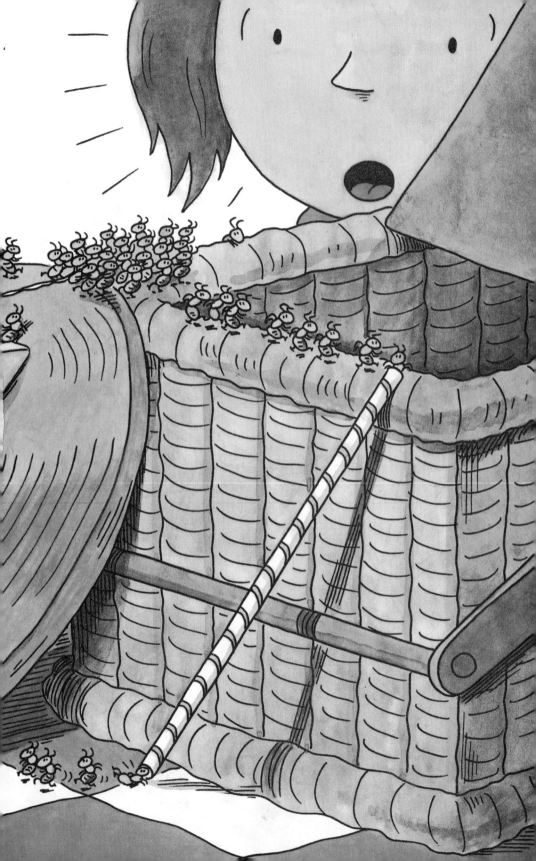

who chased the 32 with a wing and a leg,

who trailed the 16 with a hard-boiled egg,

who followed 8 ants with a crisp bacon strip,

who chased the 4 ants with a barbecued chip,

who trailed the 2 ants with some pieces of plum,

who followed 1 ant who carried a crumb,

a crumb from the basket with goodies to eat

that we packed for a picnic on Sullivan Street.

Then 256 ants yelled, "Hurray!"

They spotted a fudge-covered cake on a tray.

They pulled it and pushed it,

but all of that fudge

made the cake much too heavy —

it just wouldn't budge!

Taking the cake was such a big chore,

that those 256 doubled once more.

Then 512 ants, all ready to dine,

picked up the cake and got right in line...

They followed the 128 ants with some cheese,

who trailed 64 ants with take-out Chinese,

who chased 32 ants with a wing and a leg,

who trailed 16 ants with a hard-boiled egg,

who followed 8 ants with a crisp bacon strip,

who chased the 4 ants with a barbecued chip,

who trailed the 2 ants with some pieces of plum,

who followed 1 ant who carried a crumb,

a crumb from the basket with goodies to eat

that we packed for a picnic on Sullivan Street.

By the time we were hungry,

and ready for lunch,

our goodies were gone.

There was nothing to munch!

But the ants had a picnic

with goodies to eat,

down in their ant hole

on Sullivan Street.

The 512 Ants on Sullivan Street

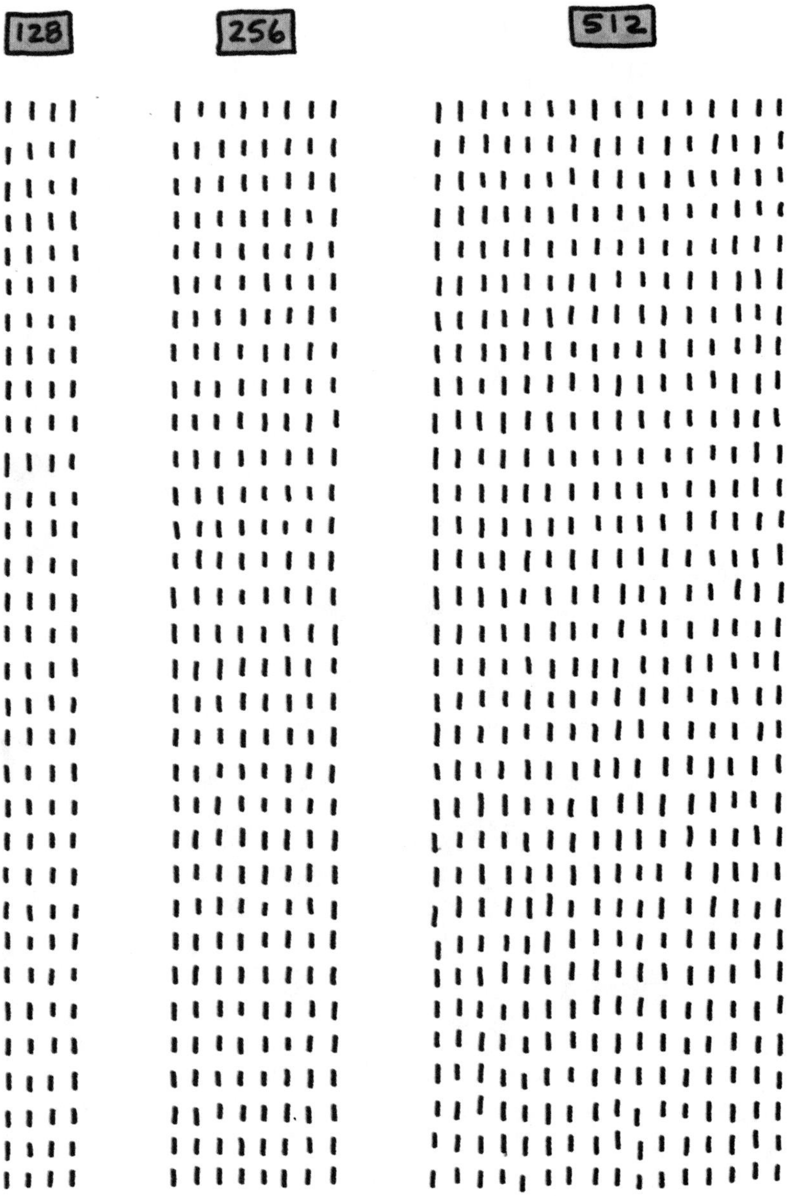
128
256
512

• About the Activities •

Number sense is an extremely important part of learning. Having number sense means understanding what you're doing when you add, subtract, multiply, and divide numbers. With this math awareness, you are able to think flexibly about numbers, see how they can be represented differently, and recognize the many ways numbers are used in the everyday world. It's the mathematical equivalent of literacy.

In order to develop number sense, children need many and varied experiences. *The 512 Ants on Sullivan Street* gives them the opportunity to think about what happens to the magnitude of numbers that double over and over again. The activities are opportunities to extend the story and engage your child in looking at how to compare numbers, see relationships among them, make appropriate estimates, and judge the reasonableness of answers from arithmetic computations. Enjoy doing the activities and talking about these ideas with your child!

— Marilyn Burns

You'll find tips and suggestions
for guiding the activities whenever
you see a box like this!

Retelling the Story

The number of ants in the story grows larger and larger. First there is 1 ant carrying a crumb, then 2 ants with some pieces of plum, followed by 4, then 8, 16, 32, 64, 128, 256, up to 512 ants. There's a pattern of doubling in these numbers. If you double one, you get two; if you double two, you get four, and so on. Another way to say that is that two is twice as much as one, four is twice as much as two, and so on.

How would you explain to someone what it means to double a number?

If the story went on, what number would come after 512? Explain how you could figure this out.

If your child can't explain either of these points, don't worry. Their math understanding is developing and children haven't thought about numbers in every way possible. If doubling is a new concept for your child, give a simple explanation yourself, reinforcing the use of "twice as many" and "double."

Ants All Over!

Look at the lines of ants on pages 40 and 41. You can use addition or multiplication to explain how the number of ants connect to one another.

Addition	**Multiplication**
1	**1**
2 = 1 + 1	**2** = 2 x 1
4 = 2 + 2	**4** = 2 x 2
8 = 4 + 4	**8** = 2 x 4
16 = 8 + 8	**16** = 2 x 8
32 = 16 + 16	**32** = 2 x 16
64 = 32 + 32	**64** = 2 x 32
128 = 64 + 64	**128** = 2 x 64
256 = 128 + 128	**256** = 2 x 128
512 = 256 + 256	**512** = 2 x 256

Can you explain how the pattern of addition explains why the numbers double?

You can read each of the multiplication sentences in two ways. One way is to use the word "times." For example, you can say, "eight equals two times four." Or you can think of eight as two groups with four in each group and say, "eight equals two groups of four." Can you use the drawing of ants to explain why this makes sense?

Ant Squares

A different way to look at how the sizes of numbers compare as they double is to put the ants in rows and columns like this.

These ant arrangements are shaped like rectangles. Some of those rectangles are squares. How many ants are in each of the squares? These numbers, 1, 4, 16, and 64, are called *square numbers*. They can be written as multiplication in a different way than you saw before. It's all how you look at and think about numbers!

$$\mathbf{1} = 1 \times 1$$
$$\mathbf{4} = 2 \times 2$$
$$\mathbf{16} = 4 \times 4$$
$$\mathbf{64} = 8 \times 8$$

See if you can read each of the sentences above in two ways, using "times" and then "groups of."

Now try your own arranging. You'll need 16 of the same small object — pennies, beans, or

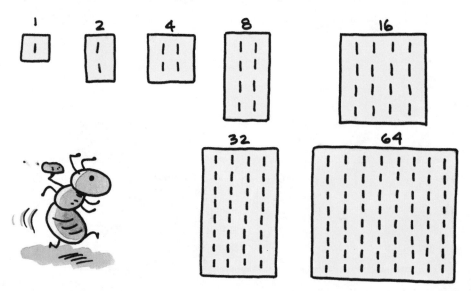

buttons will do. Arrange your 16 objects into two groups of eight (2 x 8). What shape did you make?

Next, arrange your same 16 objects into four groups of four (4 x 4). Now what shape do you have?

Did you use all 16 of your objects each time? This is a tricky activity, but it's important to know that the same number can be thought of in different ways.

Which of the other numbers — 128, 256, or 512 — would also make square shapes if they were arranged in columns and rows? How can you be sure about what you think?

Can you see how the square numbers skip numbers in the doubling pattern of 1, 2, 4, 8, 16, 32, 64? Why do you think this happens?

Your child may want to try drawing ants or some other objects to answer these last two questions. If so, using lined paper to do so will help. If you add vertical lines equally spaced, you can provide a squared grid that is even more helpful.

Go for 100!

This is a game of doubling. If you start with one, double it, and keep doubling, you get the numbers in the story: 1, 2, 4, 8, 16, 32, 64, 128, 256, 512. You skip the number 100; it never comes up.

But what if you started with another number, say three? Will you land on 100 if you double three (3 + 3 = 6) and then keep on doubling (6 + 6 = 12, 12 + 12 = 24, and so on)?

What about if you start doubling with five and keep on doubling? Will you land on 100?

Can you find numbers that you could start with, double, keep on doubling, and land exactly on 100?

And one last question: Is 100 a square number?